# BIG BU$INE$$

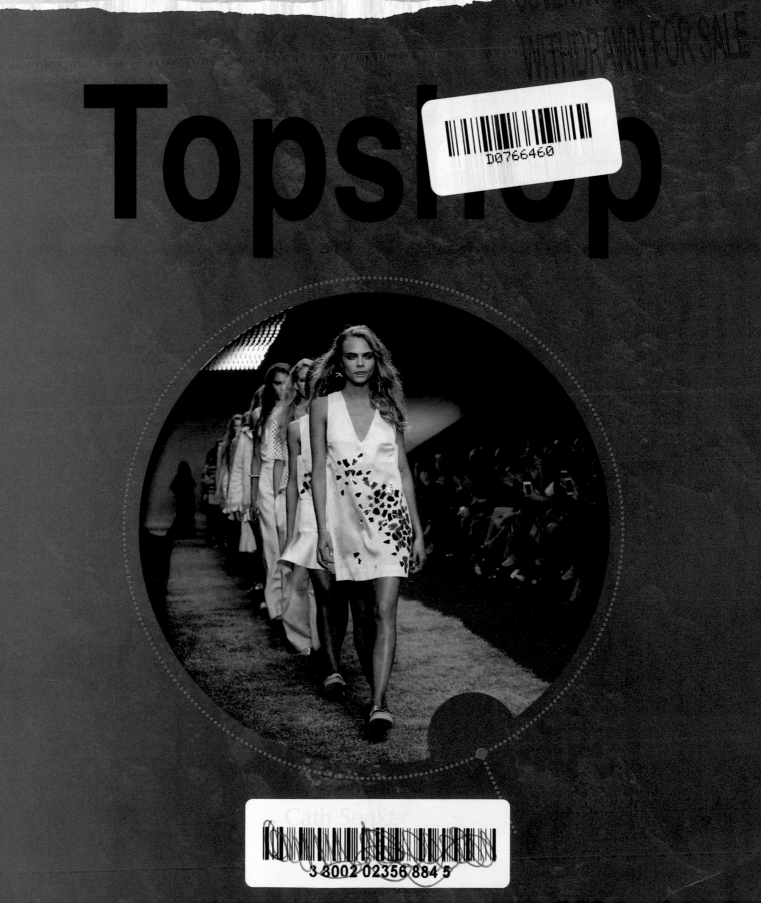

# Topshop

Cath Senker

First published in paperback in 2016 by Wayland
Copyright © Wayland 2016

Wayland
An imprint of
Hachette Children's Group
Part of Hodder & Stoughton
Carmelite House
50 Victoria Embankment
London EC4Y 0DZ

Commissioning editor: Annabel Stones
Designer: LittleRedAnt (Anthony Hannant)
Picture researcher: Shelley Noronha

ISBN: 978 0 7502 8944 3
E-book ISBN: 978 0 7502 8542 1

Dewey categorisation: 338.7'61-dc23

Printed in China

10 9 8 7 6 5 4 3 2 1

FSC
www.fsc.org

MIX
Paper from
responsible sources
FSC® C104740

Wayland is a division of Hachette Children's Group, an Hachette UK company.
www.hachette.co.uk

Picture acknowledgements: The author and publisher would like to thank the following
for allowing their pictures to be reproduced in this publication:
Cover: Simon Dawson/Bloomberg via Getty Images; title page: Shutterstock; p.4: Shutterstock; p.5:
Alex Segre / Alamy; p.6: Popperfoto/Getty Images; p.7: SSPL via Getty Images; p.8: Getty Images;
p.9: REX/Alex Segre; p. 10: KCS Presse/ /Splash News/Corbis; p.11: Shutterstock; p.12: Gamma-Rapho
via Getty Images; p.13: Getty Images; p.14: Shutterstock; p.15, top: REX/Richard Young; p. 15, bottom:
Getty Images; p.16: Getty Images; p.17 and p. 32: Shutterstock; p.18: Getty Images; p.19: AFP/Getty
Images; p.20: Shutterstock; p.21: Getty Images; p.22 Xinhua/Photoshot; p.23: AFP/Getty Images; p.24:
Getty Images; p.25: REX/Jonathan Hordle; p.26: Picture Alliance/Photoshot; p.27: WireImage.

# Contents

# Topshop today

chances are you'll spot a

...women's clothing chain...

...the UK and over 240 sh...

4

> " It is quintessentially High Street: fashionable and accessible . . . Topshop is fun, colourful and bold. It's runway stuff made affordable. "

# Burton: from humble beginnings

Topshop has its origins in a company called Burton, which was founded by an ambitious teenager! In 1900, Montague Burton, a 15-year-old Lithuanian-Jewish boy, migrated from Russia to Chesterfield, northern England. A few years later, he set up Burton, a menswear business.

In 1906 Burton began to establish a chain of stores, selling both ready-to-wear and bespoke suits, tailored for the individual. In 1910 Burton moved his business to Leeds.

World War I (1914–18) proved profitable for the Burton company, which supplied clothing for nearly a quarter of the British armed forces. During the early 1920s Montague Burton started to develop his Leeds factory; within 15 years it was the largest clothing factory in Europe.

The company even did well during the economic depression of the 1930s.

By the end of World War II (1939–45), it was estimated that 20 per cent of British men were wearing Burton clothes. In 1946 Burton moved into womenswear, buying the Peter Robinson women's fashion chain. By the time of Montague Burton's death in 1952, Burton had 616 shops and was the biggest tailoring company in the world.

*Former soldiers on their way home in 1945, some already wearing their demob suits.*

In 1945 Burton created a demob suit with shirt and tie for returning soldiers. Known as the 'Full Monty' after Montague, the suit became famous in the fashion world and gave rise to the modern saying, meaning 'absolutely everything'.

*Displaying a newly finished suit at the Burton clothing factory in Leeds.*

# Brains

## Behind The Brand

### Montague Burton
### Founder of Burton

Montague Burton left Russia with £100 to set up business in the UK. He began by peddling accessories door to door and in 1904 opened his first shop. By 1929, Burton owned 333 shops and his business took an ever-growing share of the men's clothing market.

Unlike many clothes manufacturers of the time, Burton treated his workers well. He provided meals, a dentist and an eye specialist to help needleworkers suffering with eye strain. In 1931, Burton received a knighthood for his 'services to industrial relations'. He paid close attention to detail in every department, giving clear instructions for manufacturing and sales staff. Burton's careful working methods and good treatment of his workforce led to a high quality of products and services.

In his personal life, Burton loved books and he kept up ties with the Leeds Jewish community. His success afforded him a comfortable lifestyle, and during World War II, he moved to a country house in Berkshire.

# Topshop and Topman

During the 1960s sweeping social change took place. Young people embraced new political activities, music, art and lifestyles. Along with these changes came daring new fashions, including unisex clothes such as jeans, and brightly coloured fashion. Garments were mass-produced in factories and became cheaper to buy than ever before.

*A young band wearing the brand-new jeans fashions of the 1960s.*

Against this background, the Burton company founded Topshop in 1964. At first, it was called Peter Robinson's Top Shop and was located within a department store in the Sheffield branch of the Peter Robinson chain. In the mid-1970s, Topshop became a standalone (separate) shop and soon developed into one of the leading fashion retailers on the high street. Topman was launched to attract male customers in 1978. The company continued to grow in the 1980s and 1990s. Similar to many other high-street clothes retailers, it sold the latest trends at reasonable prices.

## Business Matters

### Mergers and demergers

The Burton Group, as it was known from 1969, expanded in the 1970s by buying other fashion retailers, such as Evans (1971) and Dorothy Perkins (1979) and merging them into its business. By buying competitors' businesses, a company increases its market share and reduces competition at the same time. Another aim of a merger is to cut costs by combining departments, such as accounting and recruitment.

In 1997, the Burton Group demerged and sold its fashion retail businesses, including Topshop and Topman, to the Arcadia Group. A demerger is when a company splits into separate businesses. It allows a big company to raise money from the sale of those businesses or to divide them up to handle different interests.

In the early 1990s, Burton hired fresh young designers to improve Topshop's range. It also invested in a huge flagship store in Oxford Street, London's prime shopping location, which opened in 1994. With five floors, it was one of the largest fashion outlets in the world.

Topshop had moved upmarket from a regular retailer to a leading fashion brand.

*The front of the flagship Oxford Street Topshop.*

# Sir Philip Green: Topshop's top man

## Leveraged buy-outs

A leveraged buy-out is the purchase of a company with a large amount of borrowed money. Sir Philip Green bought companies that were performing badly for a low cost, made them profitable and then paid off the debt. After that, he gained all the profits. In 2004, Green tried to take over Marks and Spencer, but he failed to acquire this giant of the high street.

# What does Topshop offer?

Topshop offers high-fashion ranges, including a wide selection of clothing, swimwear and lingerie. The brand appeals to teenagers, students and professionals through to women in their fifties – and even celebrities.

Topshop has a variety of lines available, some affordably priced, others more exclusive. Topshop caters for women of different shapes, sizes and ages, with Tall, Petite and Maternity ranges. There's also Mini for babies. Accessories are a significant part of the business, including make-up, jewellery, bags and shoes in classic and innovative styles. Trend collections of make-up are produced each season, drawing on catwalk looks.

**Topshop Ranges:**

A model at a London fashion event showcases Topman's latest winter styles.

# Brains

## Behind The Brand

### Soulmaz Vosough
### Head of Topshop Personal Shopping

Soulmaz Vosough runs the complimentary personal shopping service for customers. Personal shoppers work with customers to hand-pick outfits for them, whether it's for a special event or to create a whole new wardrobe. The shoppers have a wide knowledge of all Topshop styles. They can help the customer to choose what will suit her or suggest how to accessorize her look with jewellery, a bag and shoes.

Vosough explains that personal shoppers build up relationships with customers and many come back regularly. They give hot tips on new collections so that the customer doesn't miss out on them. Vosough has a few style tips of her own: simply add heels to an outfit to add sophistication, or just update the silhouettes (clothing shapes) you wear and stick with the colours you love each season.

*Soulmaz Vosough (left) with fellow personal shopper Flynn Adams in Los Angeles, just before the opening of a new store in the city offering a personal shopping service.*

Topman offers a full range of clothing and suits for men. The main range follows the latest trends, and changes every month. Basic items such as T-shirts and jeans are tweaked to the current fashions. A premium collection provides refined versions, at higher prices. Topman also provides a range of suits and a Fairtrade cotton line. Topman caters to the youth market, too. It is popular with fashion-conscious teenage boys, and all Topman styles are available in extra-small sizes.

# Topshop and the fashion world

Topshop's relationship with the fashion world has propelled it to the top of the high-street retail market. It even has its own slot in the fashion calendar. In 2005, Topshop became the first high-street brand to exhibit at London Fashion Week, showing its own line, Unique.

The company first became involved with fashion designers in 2001 when it joined NEWGEN, a scheme that supports talented new designers at London Fashion Week. NEWGEN has winners every year – previous winners include top designer Alexander McQueen. Since 2003, Topshop has also sponsored Fashion East, a non-profit group that helps emerging young designers. Every year, it offers three menswear and three womenswear designers the chance to present a catwalk collection to the international press and buyers at London Fashion Week.

*Model Cara Delevingne models Topshop Unique at London Fashion Week, 2013.*

*Kate Moss launches her Topshop range, 2010.*

Topshop has worked with many well-known designers, including Christopher Kane, Jonathan Saunders and Louise Goldin. From 2007–10 the company collaborated with supermodel Kate Moss on a 'Kate Moss for Topshop' clothing line, inspired by Moss's wardrobe. This was extremely successful, and in 2013 Moss revealed she would be teaming up with Topshop again.

# ●rains
## Behind The Brand

### Kate Phelan
### Topshop's Creative Director

Kate Phelan was offered a job at quality fashion magazine *Vogue* after doing a work placement and rose to become Co-Fashion Director. After 18 years at *Vogue*, she became Creative Director at Topshop. Her role was to oversee brand identity and product development.

In 2013 Phelan worked with Google to create the first catwalk show to be fully filmed and streamed online on Topshop.com and YouTube. The team fitted high-definition micro-cameras to some of the models, so viewers had a model's-eye view of the catwalk. Viewers watching the live show could capture images and share them on social networks, and follow what was going on backstage via Instagram and Twitter. Using the Google Hangout app, fashion bloggers were invited to chat with Kate Phelan and the Topshop design team, and fans could join the discussions. The venture was hugely successful – the video stream had more than 4 million views.

*Kate Phelan in Sydney, Australia after the successful launch of a new Topshop store in the city.*

## Interacting with customers online

Having a popular and entertaining online presence allows companies to interact with their customers and find out what they want to buy. Few items displayed at fashion shows are ever made in large quantities to sell to the public. At London Fashion Week 2013, Topshop adopted a 'Be the Buyer' survey to help it decide what to manufacture. Using the Google Hangout app (see page 15), fans could indicate the items from Topshop's fashion show that they most wanted the company to produce. This helped Topshop to decide which garments to make for the shops.

...rds expanded in the real as ...ne virtual world. For example, the ...first Australian branch launched in Melbo... in 2011, and in 2012, stores in th... market opened in New...

Topshop als... wor...

# Topshop in the community

Like most big businesses, Topshop supports charities. It's good for the image of the company to be involved in the community, and many employees are keen to take part. For example, just before Christmas, Topshop staff members run a mobile soup kitchen service for Age UK, giving out soup to elderly people.

Topshop also raises money by designing special products and donating part of the proceeds to charity. For example, the company works with Fashion Targets Breast Cancer. In 2013, keyrings were produced and for each £2 sale, £1 was donated to the charity. Talented new illustrators create Christmas cards for Topshop every year, and the profits go to Age UK. By offering low-cost products, it is easy for large numbers of people to give some money to the cause.

*TV presenter Gaby Roslin (centre) at a Topshop celebrity shopping event to raise money for the Terrance Higgins Trust in 2005.*

# Business Matters

$

## Sponsorship – providing funds and support

Arcadia is an important sponsor of the Fashion Retail Academy, established in London in 2006 to provide education and training to young people who are keen to enter the fashion industry. Sir Philip Green and other Arcadia directors lead special classes, and the Academy arranges work placements and supplies information about job opportunities. As well as helping young people, the project makes excellent business sense. Supporting young people who would like to enter the industry enhances Arcadia's reputation and enables it to scoop up young talent. It may select students for work placements who go on to have high-flying careers with the company.

Charitable activities can be quite innovative. For Age Concern in 2009, Topshop created the 'dress me up' scheme. Designer dresses previously owned by celebrities, such as Peaches Geldof, Nicola Roberts and Dita von Teese, could be hired for one day for £40. The dresses were later auctioned, and all proceeds went to Age Concern.

Topman has picked charities focused on assisting men; it supports CALM, an organization that aims to reduce suicide among men under 35. Topman sponsors the charity's magazine and distributes it in stores to help the charity to reach the young men who might need support. Topshop also donates garments to charity and holds sales of sample garments at its head office to raise money.

*British Prime Minister Tony Blair meets students at the opening of the Fashion Retail Academy in 2006.*

# Topshop and tax

Topshop has enjoyed good publicity for its charitable work, but it has had negative press too. CEO Sir Philip Green has been accused of tax avoidance. He himself works in the UK and pays income tax (tax on earnings). But his wife Tina legally owns Arcadia, although she doesn't work for the company. Tina Green lives in Monaco, where it is not necessary to pay income tax.

In 2005, Sir Philip Green awarded himself a £1.2 billion dividend (sum of money from the company's profits). He put the payment through offshore accounts – bank accounts not in the UK – and it entered his wife's account in Monaco. So he didn't pay tax on it.

Campaigners against tax avoidance argued that the £285 million that Sir Philip Green failed to pay in tax could have paid for the salaries of 20,000 nurses for a year. In 2010, they protested outside Arcadia's flagship Topshop and BHS stores in central London.

" Any time it takes his fancy, Green can pay himself huge sums of money without having to pay any tax. "

UK Uncut, which campaigns against Green for not paying income tax, 2012

Demonstrators protest outside Topshop in 2011.

*Philip and Tina Green in Monaco, where Tina is a resident. Even if she earns money in the UK, she does not have to pay income tax there.*

On the other hand, Arcadia does pay corporation tax (business tax) at the full rate and has contributed £290 million a year since 2006. In contrast, around one-third of large businesses in the UK use legal methods to avoid paying as much tax as they should. Green claims that his personal finances are separate from the business and that Arcadia is more responsible than many other big firms. Sir Philip Green has said, 'We run this business 100 per cent correctly. We run it better than a public company. We know people are watching.'

## Business Matters

### Corporation tax

Corporation tax is payable on a company's profits from trade and investment, wherever in the world the money is made. It is also payable on capital gains, the profit a business makes when it sells an asset, for example, one of its companies. The rate differs, depending on how much profit the business made in the previous year. In the UK, there's a lower rate and an upper rate. Corporation tax is charged at different percentages around the world. A few countries are tax havens (they do not charge corporation tax), such as Bermuda, the Cayman islands, the Bahamas, Bahrain and the Channel Islands (including Jersey and Guernsey).

# Workers' welfare

The code of conduct states that goods must be produced without exploiting the people who made them. The company has been criticized for working with suppliers who do not treat their workers well.

> " Bangladesh's tragic factory collapse earlier this year was a wake-up call about the urgent need to improve safety standards for employees in developing countries. "

## What is Corporate Social Responsibility?

Corporate Social Responsibility (CSR) is how a company accounts for the impact of its activities on the society and environment where it operates. A company may try to reduce pollution and waste, or improve the conditions of its workers. It may back educational and social programmes in the community.

CSR can be good for business. New locations will welcome the company if it offers well-paid jobs. The company will have a better brand image, leading to more sales and attracting well-qualified staff. When employees are treated well, they tend to work hard and stay in the job.

# Raising standards

**Arcadia is making some efforts to improve workers' conditions. Here are some of the initiatives that they have been looking into.**

Arcadia opposes the practice of sand blasting, a process that gives denim a worn or faded look. One way to create the effect is for workers to fire sand at pressure onto jeans.

The sand particles break down into fine silica particles. If workers breathe them in, it can cause a fatal lung disease called silicosis.

In 2012 Topshop carried out checks at top denim suppliers' factories in Pakistan, Egypt and Turkey, and none were carrying out sand blasting.

Topshop and Topman are also working with other retailers to produce guidelines for factories employing home workers. These employees work for a company from home, for example sewing garments. They are paid a fixed amount per item. Home workers are often paid low rates – it is hard for individuals to argue with a company for more pay, and they usually need the work. The guidelines indicate that these workers should be paid a decent rate.

*Sand blasting denim to give it a 'worn' look brings great health risks for the workers, but a lot of factories still use this practice.*

Fairtrade is another way of improving working conditions. Topshop uses Fairtrade cotton for some of its clothes, such as the MOTO jeans range. This means that the workers who produce the cotton receive a fair rate and the process does not damage the environment. Fairtrade items make up a tiny proportion of Topshop's products, but the company aims to scale up Fairtrade production.

## Business Matters

$

## Animal welfare

Acting ethically can be good for a company's image. Topshop does not sell items containing exotic animal skins or fur. In 2013 the company worked with People for the Ethical Treatment of Animals (PETA) on a high-profile campaign to stop manufacturers from using the skins of animals such as snakes, alligators and lizards to make handbags and shoes. A large sign was put up in the Oxford Street store window stating 'Keep wildlife out of your wardrobe'. Topshop asked customers to pledge not to buy such items.

Window display promoting animal welfare in Topshop's Oxford Street store.

KEEP WILDLIFE OUT OF YOUR WARDROBE

OPSHOP IN SUPPORTING PETA. PLEDGE NEVER TO BUY EX    KINS A

# A future at the top

So what does the future hold for Topshop? Outside Britain, Topshop has a huge fan base. In 2013, there were plans to open 150 more franchise stores around the world, including in China, the USA, Canada, Vietnam, Australia and New Zealand.

Topshop has different strategies for expansion. In Germany and the USA, it is growing by establishing Topshop and Topman outlets in department stores. In 2013, it was announced that both shops would launch in Karstadt department stores in Germany. Topshop and Topman opened in 14 Nordstrom department stores in the USA in 2012 and were to enter 28 more by the end of 2013. Arcadia also planned to introduce five new standalone Topshop and Topman shops to US cities.

*A Topshop display in the Düsseldorf Karstadt department store, Germany.*

In the Far East, Topshop is entering the developing market for mid-range stores. For example, Hong Kong used to have high-quality luxury shops and cheap, basic clothing shops but few outlets catering to the middle ground. Topshop has joined companies such as Marks and Spencer, Burberry and Timberland that have set up in Hong Kong to fill this gap in the market. In 2013 Topshop was working towards opening stores in mainland China too.

> " A great team leading these brands, a lot of hard work, and this constant stream of fresh must-have pieces gives us the confidence to continue to push on internationally, both with our franchise partners and with our search for our own fully owned flagships. "

Sir Philip Green, 2013

# Brains

## Behind The Brand

### Mary Homer
### Managing Director of Topshop

Mary Homer became Managing Director in 2006, having worked for Arcadia for 22 years. During the first couple of years, she successfully oversaw Topshop's launch in New York and its expansion in Russia and the Far East. She led the push into Australia, with the opening of stores in Melbourne (2011) and Sydney (2012) in partnership with a local franchise company. She was confident that Topshop could adapt its ranges to cope with the different seasons there. In 2013, Homer was promoting Topshop's grand plans to extend its presence across Asia, using social media to promote the brand in mainland China.

Mary Homer believes Topshop will be popular with Chinese shoppers.

[When designing a new product it is helpful to put together a product development brief like the one below. Try this exercise. Name your junior...]

## Product Development Brief

......................................................●

**Name of product:** Topshop Fashion Juniors.

**Design of logo:**

**The product explained (use 25 words or less):**
A fashion range for boys and girls aged 9–14 who love to wear up-to-the-minute styles.

**Target age of users:** 9–14.

**What is the product?:** This affordable range has the latest fashion basics, such as trousers, jeans, shirts, T-shirts, skirts and dresses, adapted for kids and young teens.

**Are there any similar products available?:** None that I know of.

**What makes your product different?:** The range brings Topshop styles to younger customers.

●.........................................

# SWOT Analysis
## (Strengths, Weaknesses, Opportunities and Threats)

... are assessing ...
... Juniors

The information below will help you ass...
can make your product stron...

## Questions to consider

### Strengths

Does your product do something unique?
What are its USPs? (unique selling points)
Why will people buy this range rather than a different one?

Yes. There is no other Topshop range for this age group.

Topshop is the only high-street retailer to exhibit at London Fashion Week. Catwalk looks, tailored for young bodies, will be available to pre-teens and young teens.

Topshop is hugely appealing to young people and will attract fashion-conscious kids.

### Weaknesses

Why wouldn't people buy this range?
Does it live up to the claims you make?
Is it as good or better than other ranges already available?

Other high-street retailers such as H&M and Zara have cheaper fashion ranges for the 9–14 age group.

The range would need to be tried out on a focus group to check that the high-fashion garments suit young bodies.

This range would need to stand out and be reasonably priced to sell well.

### Opportunities

Can the range be expanded in the future, for example, to include outerwear and underwear?
Will new markets emerge for this range?
Can it be sold globally?
Can it develop new USPs?

Yes. If the range proves popular, it will be relatively easy to expand it.

Topshop and Topman are expanding overseas, and the new range could be sold into the new markets.

Yes – as above.

Topshop could employ new designers to create garments tailored to the 9–14 age group.

### Threats

Are there already too many fashion retailers in the market?
Is the market for high-fashion children's clothing less developed in Topshop's growing international markets?
Is it the right time to launch the new range?
Are any of the weaknesses so bad that they might affect the success of the venture in the long term?

There may not be a big enough market for another mid-range fashion collection.

The appeal of Topshop Fashion Juniors may be more limited in the Far East and Middle East than in Western countries.

Topshop is already engaged in international expansion so it might be a bad time to launch a new fashion range.

No. Topshop has huge production and sales capacity so the risks of producing a small range to test the waters are not great.

# Do you have what it takes to work at Topshop or Topman?
## Try this quiz!

**1) Do you enjoy shopping?**

a) No! I can't think of anything more boring than traipsing around shops.

b) Yes, I like checking out the latest trends.

c) A shopping centre is my idea of heaven. I could shop 24/7.

**2) What's your taste in clothes like?**

a) I'm not fussed about my clothes. I'm quite happy to wear hand-me-downs or let my parents buy my outfits.

b) I keep up with the latest styles and update my wardrobe regularly.

c) I'm obsessed with fashion! I'm constantly on the watch for the next new look and can't wait to buy it.

**3) Would you describe yourself as creative?**

a) No, not really.

b) I appreciate good style and I enjoy arts and crafts activities.

c) Yes. I love drawing different outfits and looks. I fancy myself as a designer – I'm always changing my bedroom round.

**4) Which job environment would you prefer?**

a) I'd like a nice, quiet job in an office.

b) I'd prefer to be up and about and on my feet.

c) My ideal job would be working in a massive clothes store.

**5) Would you like to work with people?**

a) No. I'm shy and I don't like talking to people I don't know.

b) Yes, I enjoy being around other people.

c) I'm a chatty type, so I'd love a job where I'm paid to talk all day.

**6) Are you good at working with others?**

a) No. I'm not keen on working in groups at school. I prefer to do my own thing.

b) Yes – I'm always the one who gathers a group together to play games at break.

c) Yes – I get on with everyone and people always ask me to help to sort out problems with friends.

**7) What are your energy levels like?**

a) I'm a bit of a couch potato – I prefer quiet pastimes.

b) I'm pretty active. I join in with sports and different activities.

c). I'm on the go the whole time. I love to keep busy.

# Results

**Mostly As:** It doesn't look like you're suited to the retail business. You'd need to be more energetic and prepared to work with people. If you're really keen on working for Topshop or Topman, when you're older you could try doing some work experience in a charity shop to see how you get on in a shop environment.

**Mostly Bs:** You clearly have some interest in fashion and working with people, so shop work might suit you. When you're older, you might like to look for a job as a sales advisor and take it from there.

**Mostly Cs:** You're creative, energetic and you love fashion. If you keep up those interests, you have the potential to work at the Topshop flagship store or to be a manager in the retail business.

# Glossary

**asset** something of value that a person or company owns, and that can be used or sold

**auctioned** sold to the person who offers the most money for the item at an auction – a public event to sell things

**bespoke** made specially for an individual customer

**brand** a product made by a particular company; for example, Arcadia has several brands, including Topshop (women's clothing) and Topman (men's clothing)

**chain** a group of stores owned by the same company

**classic** simple and traditional in style, not affected by changes in fashion

**collaboration** working with another person or group to produce something together, such as a fashion collection

**concession** the right to sell products in an area that is part of a larger store

**demerger** the act of separating a company from a larger company

**department store** a large store that is divided into several parts, each part selling a different type of goods

**depression** a period when there is little economic activity and many people have no work

**ethical** to do with beliefs about what is right and wrong. In business, acting ethically usually means treating workers fairly and not harming the environment or wildlife.

**exclusive** of high quality and expensive and therefore not often bought or used by most people

**fairtrade** involving trade that supports producers in poor countries by paying fair prices and making sure that the workers have good working conditions and fair pay

**flagship store** the most important store that a company owns

**franchise** permission given by a company to somebody who wants to sell its goods or services in a particular area

**import** a product or service that is brought into one country from another

**innovative** new and original ways of doing things

**invest** to spend money on something in order to make it better or more successful

**knighthood** in the UK, an award that is given for services to the country

**leveraged buy-out** borrowing money to buy a company

**merger** the act of joining two or more organizations or businesses into one

**mid-range stores** stores that sell items in the middle of the price range – neither the cheapest goods nor top-quality designer items

**minimum wage** the lowest wage that an employer is allowed to pay by law

**premium** selling at a higher price than normal

**ready-to-wear** made in standard sizes, not to the measurements of a particular customer

**recruitment** finding new people to join a company

**sponsorship** providing funds and support, for example, for a charity or for education

**standalone store** a store that operates alone rather than as part of a department store

**supply chain** the series of processes involved in the production and supply of goods, from when they are first made until they are bought or used

**tax avoidance** ways of paying only the smallest amount of tax that you legally have to

**Trade Union** an organization of workers, usually in a particular industry, that exists to improve their working conditions and pay

# Index